We played and protected each other like the Three Musketeers because I was . . .

# TORTURED
# IN MY
# OWN HOME

On Newsstands Now:

**TRUE STORY**
and
**TRUE CONFESSIONS**
Magazines

*True Story* and *True Confessions* are the world's largest and best-selling women's romance magazines. They offer true-to-life stories to which women can relate.

Since 1919, the iconic *True Story* has been an extraordinary publication. The magazine gets its inspiration from the hearts and minds of women, and touches on those things in life that a woman holds close to her heart, like love, loss, family and friendship.

*True Confessions*, a cherished classic first published in 1922, looks into women's souls and reveals their deepest secrets.

---

To subscribe, please visit our website:
**www.TrueRenditionsLLC.com** or call **(212) 922-9244**

To find the TRUES at your local store, please visit:
**www.WheresMyMagazine.com**

We played and protected each other like the Three Musketeers because I was . . .

# TORTURED IN MY OWN HOME

From the Editors
Of *True Story* And
*True Confessions*

Published by True Renditions, LLC


True Renditions, LLC
105 E. 34th Street, Suite 141
New York, NY 10016

ISBN: 978-1-938877-74-2

Visit us on the web at www.truerenditionsllc.com.

# Chapter 1

I'd never known that shadows could be so deep—or that the silence could be so loud. I didn't dare to turn on the flashlight that I had in my pocket. I was afraid that Albert might have seen the glimmer of light shining through the dirt-smudged windows of the small storage room above the garage. I was suddenly afraid that I'd made a mistake in hiding up there. I realized that maybe I should have stayed in the house. Would I have been safer there? No, I knew that I could have died there. So, I had escaped the danger and, like a coward, I was hiding in the dark in that lonely, horrible room. I couldn't believe that my life had come to that moment—that I'd been reduced to the need to hide there, praying that no one would find me.

I hated that place—and, yet, it had been a sanctuary for me, and for Albert. How many times had we climbed up the tall woodpile behind the garage and scrambled through the rear window into that musty place? It had been our only refuge from Mama's rages when we'd been children.

I could remember hearing her high-pitched voice yelling at my brother. "Albert!" she'd screamed. "Get in here! Right now!"

Would I have been safer there? No, I knew that I could have died there. So, I had escaped the danger and, like a coward, I was hiding in the dark in that lonely, horrible room. I couldn't believe that my life had come to that moment—that I'd been reduced to the need to hide there, praying that no one would find me.

I hated that place—and, yet, it had been a sanctuary for me, and for Albert. How many times had we climbed up the tall woodpile behind the garage and scrambled through the rear window into that musty place? It had been our only refuge from Mama's rages when we'd been children.

I could remember hearing her high-pitched voice yelling at my brother. "Albert!" she'd screamed. "Get in here! Right now!"

No matter what he had been doing outside, he'd gone racing into the house, his young face betraying his fear of what Mama would scold him for that time. And, inevitably, there was always something that one of us was ordered to do—or, that we'd already done wrong.

"Albert, get that mud swept off the back porch!" she'd yell. "When you're done with that, go down into the basement and bring up more canning jars for me. And, hurry up about it!"

Her list of orders and demands was endless and, no matter how hard Albert or I tried, what we did was never good enough to suit

Mama. Our best efforts still brought her wrath storming down upon us. I'd tried so hard to please her—to do exactly what she'd wanted me to do in exactly the way that she'd wanted it done. All that my sincere efforts had earned me was only a harsh reprimand because, according to her, I hadn't done the job right.

I didn't wash the dishes correctly and I didn't run the vacuum in the right way and I didn't scrub the bathtub thoroughly enough. Then, I would be sent to my room, or I would be denied television, or dessert. And, of course, I would be given extra work to do to make up for the not-good-enough jobs that I had already completed.

Mama had always seemed to have been driven by some horrible anger, deep within her. Her eyes sometimes filled with tears for no reason, and her hands shook. Often, she tensed up and, sometimes, she wrapped her arms around herself—it was as if she were trying to hold herself together. And, she clenched her teeth—sort of grinding them as her jaw tensed. That was often the final signal that her rage had begun to spiral out of control. I'd learned to recognize those movements and actions as warning signals. They were almost always followed by her rages—by her displays of intense anger at my brother or me.

# Chapter 2

As we got older and became teenagers, the situation escalated. I'd seen Mama standing at the kitchen sink doing dishes—just a routine, daily job. Her shoulders would tense, she'd throw a cup or bowl into the sink, and then, she'd whirl around. Her eyes would be flashing—filled with something unspeakable. Once, before I could react or intercede, she'd grabbed a cereal bowl and hurled it at Albert, hitting him on the arm.

Startled, he'd yelped and clutched at his arm.

"Get out! Get out!" she'd screamed. He'd run, terrified, wondering what she would throw at him next. When he ran, I ran, too. I knew that it would only be a matter of moments before she'd throw something at me—and she seldom missed.

Sometimes, when I had been helping her in the kitchen, she'd grab my arm, whirl me around to face her, and shake me. There was no way that I could have fended off her attacks, because at those times, she seemed to have had extra strength. When she'd finally released me, I'd darted from the kitchen and fled up the steps to my room, where I'd thrown myself across my bed and cried.

Or, I'd followed my brother's example and had escaped through the back door. As quickly as I possibly could, I'd raced to the back of the garage, scrambled up the woodpile, and climbed in through the window. Then, I'd dropped down onto the floor, my chest heaving from the shock of Mama's assault, and from the effort of scrambling up the woodpile to reach a safe place. In time, Albert would come to me and put his arms around me. Sometimes, we cried together. Sometimes, our agony was beyond tears, and we just huddled together—glad that the latest session of terror was over. But, we'd always wondered how soon—and how severe—the next one would be.

Not all of Mama's rages were as extreme, but they'd always had a major impact on my brother and me. We'd always been made to feel inadequate—never good enough, never capable enough.

I knew that I'd never forget the time when Albert had been about twelve years old. Mama had told him to go out to the garage, get a can of paint, and paint the fence out back. So, he'd done just as he was told, and when he'd finished, I'd thought that he'd done a great job. The fence had looked so fresh and nice—just like new. I had been so proud of how well Albert had completed his assignment.

"She's definitely going to like this," I promised my brother.

"No, she won't, Constance," he mumbled as he picked up the

empty paint can to carry it back to the garage. "She'll just say that I've done it all wrong. Then she'll scream, and she'll make me do it all over again."

I saw tears in his eyes as he headed across the yard, and I also saw the defeated slump of his shoulders.

And, of course, Albert had been right. When Mama had looked at the fence, she'd began to find fault with my brother's work immediately.

"You missed a spot there!" She pointed to a small place on the fence. "And you let the paint drip here." She pointed to a few drops of paint that had dripped onto the ground from his brush. "Can't you ever do anything right!" Her voice had begun to rise shrilly, accenting each word that she said.

"But, Mama, it looks fine. Albert did a real good job." I tried to defend my brother. I truly thought that he'd done an excellent job of painting.

"If you consider a half-done job good—then, I guess it's good," she said sarcastically. Then, she went back into the kitchen, slamming the screen door behind her.

It's amazing, I thought as she disappeared into the kitchen. If she slams the screen door, it's okay, but if Albert or I do it, then it's a real crime. And then, she grabs the wooden spoon and she comes after us. Why is it all right for her—but all wrong for us?

That wretched wooden spoon—how I'd hated that thing! She'd used it for everything—mixing pancakes, stirring a pot of stew on the stove, preparing a bowl of macaroni salad. But, mostly, she'd used the spoon on Albert and me. She had a way of reaching for that long-handled spoon and swiping out at us for any small infraction of her long list of rules. She'd come at us, wildly waving that awful weapon. When she'd managed to get within striking distance of us, we'd felt the pain of the sharp blows as the spoon had landed on our legs, arms, or backs. I'd often worn long-sleeved blouses to hide the bruises that my own mother had inflicted upon me.

Often, we'd had no idea why she'd hit us—we hadn't know what had angered her that time. We'd just turned and run—always in a different direction. We'd never run directly to the back of the garage for fear that she would catch on to the fact that we used the high stack of wood as a way to get up there. Once we'd climbed through the window, we'd always felt safe—at least for a while.

4

# Chapter 3

And yet, there was another side to Mama. When she was in one of her good moods, she could be sweet and funny. I'd always believed that that was when she'd tried to make up for the not-so-good times. She and I had baked cookies together. Sometimes, she'd set me on a kitchen chair and trimmed my hair, making it look soft and pretty. One time, she'd even made me a new dress. I had been so proud when I'd worn it to church. It had been very special to me because Mama had made it herself—during one of her good times.

When she was having one of her good days, Mama helped Albert with his homework, patiently explaining his assignments to him. When he'd managed to grasp what she'd been telling him and had completed his assignments, she'd told him that she was proud of him and made him hot chocolate as a reward.

But, sadly, those good times had been rare. Most of the time, I had felt as though I had been walking on a tightrope—afraid that if I made one false step, I would be in major trouble with Mama. At times like that, the upstairs garage room was the only place that I knew to go—where I could safely escape the wrath of my mother.

At the far end of the room, there was an opening, from which was suspended a wooden ladder. My father had used the ladder to climb up there to store tools, old pieces of cast-off furniture, and excess lumber. But, when his arthritis had gotten worse, he hadn't been able to climb the ladder any longer, so he hadn't been able to get to us.

When we'd eventually felt that it was safe, Albert and I would move cautiously down the rickety ladder and leave through the front door of the old garage. Our parents had never guessed where we had actually been. And, we had made a solemn vow to one another never to tell them. It was our secret.

Ironically, my brother and I had also had fun in our secret room. On rainy days, we'd climbed up there, sat on the floor, and had played hilarious games of checkers and chess. We'd acted silly—giggling and playing checkers in a fast-and-furious fashion. I'd realized, years later, that our exaggerated silliness had been a form of release from the pent-up fears that had lived deep within both of us. But, oh, how we'd laughed—so hard! We'd had to be sure to stifle our laughter because we didn't want our parents to hear us if they'd happened to come into the garage while we had been up there. Trying not to laugh had just made us laugh harder. I believed that our craziness had been a release valve that had kept both of us sane.

Our house was on an out-of-the way country road. Only a few other houses had been scattered along the road. Across from us had been the small white house where Mrs. Monroe and her son, Gil, lived. Gil was the same age as Albert so, at least, my brother and I had someone to play with. Sometimes, they hadn't wanted a younger girl tagging along with them when they went across the field or off to the river with their fishing poles. But, most of the time, they'd put up with me and allowed me to join in their fun.

Albert and Gil had started high school a year before I had, and they'd graduated a year before I had. It had always seemed as though Albert always got to do things before I did—including leaving home. A week after his graduation, Albert told our parents that he was signing on with the traveling carnival that had been set up on the edge of our small town.

"Why are you going to work with a carnival?" Dad demanded as we all sat at the supper table. "You can't get ahead in life, working with a carnival. There's no money in that kind of work."

"Albert, you don't really want to go off with those types," Mama added in her whining voice. "Goodness only knows what kind of people belong to that group."

"Besides, I'd thought that you were planning to stay here and help me to take care of the place," Dad reminded him. "You know that I can't do all of the work here myself. And, Constance can't help with the heavy chores—working in the garden or chopping wood. It takes a strong, young man to do that kind of work."

"Not to mention that I need Constance to help me here in the house," Mama insisted. "You have no choice. You've got stay, Albert, and help your father." There had been a note of finality in her tone.

Albert had said nothing. He'd just sat there, eating his supper and staring at the faded, worn cloth that had covered the battered table.

After I'd helped Mama with the dishes, I had gone out to sit on the back porch. I could see out across the yard, beyond the weathered garage and garden. I had always despised all the hard work that the garden had required of me. I'd always considered it an ugly weed patch—never a beautiful garden.

Next, I'd glanced in the other direction. I saw the wooded area where my father cut logs to provide heat for our house in the winter. Everyone else had a gas furnace by then—but, not for us—not for the Harbinger family. We still had an ugly, old wood-and-coal-burning furnace in the basement and it was always hungry for more wood. So, the woodpile had always being stacked high with logs.

As I'd scanned the property, I'd seen no sign of Albert. Where was he? I'd wanted to talk to him about his plans to leave with the carnival. Then, suddenly, I'd realized where he was.

6

Walking slowly so that I wouldn't draw attention to myself, I'd headed toward the garage. In case my parents were watching, I'd moved beyond the garage to the edge of the garden. Then, I'd knelt down and yanked a few weeds from between some young plants. What I'd done was a "normal" action—one that would not cause my parents to suspect anything suspicious.

After a moment, I'd surreptitiously moved behind the garage and quickly scrambled up the stack of wood. Albert had always helped my father with the woodpile, so he'd intentionally arranged it in a way that allowed easy access to the window above. Thanks to him, I was able to get up the stack quickly, push open the window, and drop down onto the floor.

Just as I'd suspected, Albert was already up there, sitting on an old crate that we'd pushed close to the wall.

"What took you so long?" he asked quietly.

"Albert, are you really going to leave with the carnival?" I asked as I sat down beside him.

"Yes." There was a note of finality to his response.

"But, why?" I really wanted to know. "You can't just leave here—"

"I will leave here," he stated flatly. "I can't stand their abuse anymore. And, that wooden spoon—Mama still hits me with that stupid thing!"

"I know. It's terrible. Everyone at the church thinks that our mother is such a wonderful woman. If they only knew what we've have had to endure for so many years. But, no one knows," I lamented.

"One person knows," Albert corrected me. "Gil knows. He's seen her hit me with that spoon, and he's heard her yelling at me. He knows that no matter how hard I work, it's never going to be good enough for her—or for Dad. He's heard Dad ordering me to do more and more of the work around here. He thinks that they're horrible parents—and he's right."

"Is Gil going with you?" I asked. I suddenly realized that, with my brother leaving, I would really be alone in this horrific situation. If Gil left, too, I would have felt as though I had been truly abandoned.

"No, Gil isn't going with me. I've tried to talk him into it, but he's staying here. He's planning to go and work at the factory. But, there's no way that I'm working there. There's no future in working at that noisy, dirty place—that's for sure."

I felt a slight relief after I'd learned that Gil would still be across the road.

"But, Albert, everyone goes to work at the factory," I reminded my brother. "That's all there is around here—just the factory."

"You're right," he agreed. "That's why I'm getting out of here—

7

that, and the fact that Mama and Dad are so awful."

We sat silently awhile, each of us considering the future. What he was planning was a bold move for Albert, and I was frightened for him. How would he manage, traveling with the carnival? Mama had often told us that those people were not to be trusted. Would he be safe? And yet, I felt proud of him, too, because he'd had the courage to take a stand—to step out of the unhappy life that we had always known.

"Do you have everything?" I asked finally.

"Yes." He nodded and pointed to the old, battered bag that he'd pushed into the shadows. Dad never could understand what had happened to the old bag that he'd used for camping so many years before. But, Albert and I had always known—my brother and I had "borrowed" it.

We'd both figured that this day would come eventually. Albert had vowed that he'd leave home one day. I'd understood, but I hadn't wanted the day to come, because it would mean that I would lose my brother—my only sense of security. Just in case things got too bad at home, Albert and I had begun to collect a few supplies, which we'd kept in the crate. My brother had a couple of worn shirts, and an old pair of pants, and some socks that I'd mended for him. There was also a flashlight and some cans of food. And, there was a tattered purse with a small amount of money that we'd managed to hide away.

"I don't want you to go," I whispered, afraid that I was going to cry.

He stood up and glanced around. "Thank goodness that we've had this place," he murmured, half to himself. "No one else knows about it—and, don't you let anyone know about it. It's your only safe place, Constance."

"Does Gil know?" I asked.

He nodded. "I showed it to him a couple of years ago, and we've come up here a few times. But, you can trust him. He'll never tell anyone about it." Albert paused, as though considering something, then continued. "Constance, if you ever need anything at all—if it gets to be too much, or you're afraid, or in danger—you can always go across the road to Gil. He'll help you. You can trust him," he assured me.

There was an awkward silence. Neither of us knew what to say or do next. I glanced at my brother and, suddenly, I realized that the gangly, awkward kid who who'd chased me across the fields, who teased me with bugs, and who'd threatened to throw me into the river, was no longer a kid. He was a young man. When had he grown up? For the first time, I saw that my brother had become a man, and I realized that his eyes held a look of fierce determination.

In that moment, I knew that he would never be the same again. He was leaving—leaving me behind, leaving his boyhood behind. I wanted to scream at him, and beg him to stay with me. But, I also knew that he had to do what he had to do. So, I said nothing.

I stood up then and walked to the other side of the room. Slowly, I made my way down the ladder. I didn't look back. I moved out of the garage into the late afternoon sun. I knew in my heart that nothing was ever going to be the same again.

# Chapter 4

When I woke up the next morning, Albert was gone. I couldn't believe how angry my parents were at his having had the nerve to defy them enough to leave. And, I couldn't believe how much I missed Albert. I moved through the next few days automatically. I helped my mother with the housework, and I helped my father with the garden. Once Albert had gone, it seemed as though there was no end to all the extra work that they'd expected me to do.

I'd felt a rising anger at my parents for their pushing at me to do more—to get more things done. Although some of the fire was gone from my mother's attitude, she still screamed at me, and she still grabbed me roughly. I'd always made sure never to be near the basement steps when she was close to me. I didn't want to go tumbling down into the cold, dark basement.

I didn't think that my parents had actually believed that Albert would ever leave home. Once he'd gone, a change had come over my parents. They seemed older, suddenly. Dad's shoulders seemed more stooped, and he walked more slowly because his arthritis had made him ache all over. Mama sat in her rocking chair more often—mending or reading, or just staring off into space.

One night, a couple of weeks after Albert had left, I'd overheard my parents talking as they'd sat on the back porch.

"It isn't right—him going off like he did," Dad mumbled. "He should have stayed here. He should be helping me around this place."

"I never thought that he would actually go," Mama said quietly. There was no anger in her voice—just a sort of sad disbelief. "I've thought a lot about all of this," she continued. "I guess I was too hard him—demanded too much of him. I was too strict."

"But, you have to be strict with children," Dad reasoned. "You have to teach them right from wrong. You have to tell them what to do and what not to do. If you don't, they'll grow up with no respect for their elders—no desire to work."

"Albert was a good boy," Mama reminded him. "He worked hard—all the time. Maybe he worked too hard. He never had the time to run and play like children should. I know that I scolded at him too much. I only wanted to train him—to teach him the proper way to behave. But, I guess I went too far. It's my fault that he left. I drove him away." She sobbed. "I drove my own son away from his home and family. I shouldn't have yelled at him so often."

"If you spare the rod, you spoil the child," Dad told her. "That's what the Bible teaches us."

"That might be true," Mama agreed. "But there is also a passage in the Bible that says, 'A gentle answer turns away wrath, but a harsh word stirs up anger.' I never had gentle words for Albert. All I ever did was chastise him. I've been thinking a lot about this. I feel as though I drove my own boy away." I heard her voice break with grief. "I never meant to do that, but

I realize now that that's just what I did."

I wasn't sure of what else they said because I turned from the doorway. I went upstairs, threw myself across my bed, and cried a river of tears.

# Chapter 5

Somehow, I got through that summer. There was one advantage to the extra work that Mama had piled upon me—it kept me too busy to have time to think about how miserable I was. And, I had no time to dwell on how much I missed my brother. The only time that I had off was on Sunday mornings, when I went to church with my parents. I sat in the front section with the other teenagers, but I didn't linger after the service to chat with them because Dad always wanted to hurry home.

I saw Gil and his mother at church often. I'd look across the aisle at Sadie Monroe, who'd be sitting there with a smile on her pretty face. I could hear her clear voice as she sang the hymns. Why can't Mama be like that? I wondered. Why did she have to be so harsh—so demanding? Why did she have to be so miserable—and make everyone around her miserable, too? I envied Gil. He was lucky to have such a nice mother.

I saw him sitting beside his mother and realized that he, like my brother, had changed. He was no longer the kid who'd liked to pull my hair or who'd dared me to climb onto the roof. He'd changed—just like Albert had changed. And, I began to realize that I had changed, too. That realization was somewhat unnerving. Everything was different, all of sudden. And I wasn't sure if I liked that.

I seldom got to talk with Gil because his days were spent working at the factory and his evenings were filled with things that he did for his mother—taking care of her large vegetable garden, or mowing the wide expanse of lawn. One time, I saw him doing something to the gutters on his mother's house. I waved at him, and he waved back. And, for some reason, his gesture had made me feel very special.

The start of my final year of school meant that I had less housework, but a lot of schoolwork. I struggled with some of my classes, as I was trying hard to get good grades. I thought that, maybe, if my grades were good enough, then Mama would be pleased with me. Maybe. . . .

Somehow, I got through the long, cold winter months. I couldn't recall ever having experienced such deep, biting cold before—such relentless blasts of wind-driven snow. I waded through high drifts to get to the end of the driveway, where I caught the school bus. I was so cold all of the time. I couldn't even remember what it felt like to be warm. I hated winter—especially that winter.

But, eventually, spring brought a fresh green look to the landscape. I was kept very busy with all of the last-minute details prior to graduation.

On a lovely spring evening, I walked across the high school stage with the rest of my classmates and received my diploma. I was very proud—and yet, I felt badly that Albert wasn't there to share in my special moment with me. The once-in-a-lifetime event was less special because my brother wasn't there.

Behind my smiles were unshed tears for the brother that I missed so much. It seemed so long ago since he'd walked away from our home—from my life. There'd been no word from him in the months since his departure. I wondered if he was all right—if he was safe. I wondered if he was even alive. Most of all, I wondered if he missed me as much as I missed him.

Several days later, my life took a drastic turn. Mama became ill—she felt disoriented, and she staggered a little when she walked. She sat at the kitchen table and cried softly. Although she'd always been so harsh, it bothered me to see her like that—a defeated person.

I had been fixing Mama a cup of tea, hoping that it would help to calm her. At the sound of someone walking across the back porch and then, a light rapping on the door, I glanced up to see Sadie Monroe. She didn't often come across the road to see Mama. I'd always felt as though she'd actually tried to avoid Mama. And, to be honest, I couldn't blame her.

"Mrs. Monroe, come on in," I invited cordially, after I'd set the cup of tea in front of my mother. I was acting as though we had company every day—instead of almost never. "I just made Mama a cup of tea. Would you like one?" I offered.

Sadie stepped into the kitchen, closing the door gently behind her. "A cup of tea?" She smiled. "Well—yes, that would be nice."

"Here, have a seat." I pulled out a chair for her opposite Mama. "I'll get the tea for you."

"Hello, Josephine," she said as she looked at Mama. Then Sadie looked at me—and there was a question in her eyes. She could see that something was very wrong.

I was standing behind Mama, and I just shrugged my shoulders. I was trying to tell her, without words, that I knew that something was not right with Mama, but that I didn't know what it was.

Sadie took charge of the situation. She accepted the tea that I placed on the table in front of her. She began chatting with Mama, talking about how well the garden was growing, about a new skirt that she'd bought—idle conversation. But, Mama didn't respond. She just sat there, ignoring the tea, and ignoring Sadie Monroe.

After a few minutes, Sadie got up from the table, said good-bye to Mama, and walked out the back door. She signaled for me to follow her.

When we were out on the back porch, she turned to me. "Is your mother all right?" she asked, a note of concern in her voice.

I shook my head. "I don't know what's wrong with her. She just sits there," I explained.

"What about her rages?" Sadie asked. I was stunned to think that Sadie Monroe knew about Mama's temper. Seeing my expression, she took my hands in hers. "Constance, I can hear your mother clear over at my house."

It had never occurred to me that Sadie knew our family secret.

She stood looking at me, compassion in her eyes. "Look, honey, I realize that it's difficult for you. I also realize that there is something seriously wrong with your mother. You need to get her to a doctor—right away."

Her words frightened me. Why should I have to take Mama to see a doctor?

Sadie gave me a hug. "Don't be upset. Just get her to a doctor and let him examine her. It's very possible that he can help her." She started down the porch steps. Glancing back at me, she continued. "If you need me, I'm just across the road."

# Chapter 6

The next day, I took Mama to see Dr. Cortland. After he'd spent some time with Mama, he told me that she was suffering from what he called "mood swings." He used terms such as "body chemistry imbalance," "anxiety," and "depression." I didn't fully understand what it was that he was trying to tell me. He wasn't very good at explaining things. But, he gave me pills to give to Mama and he explained that she had to take the pills every day. If she did, he said that the moods and the rages would be controlled. If she didn't take the pills, he told us that things would just get worse.

Dr. Cortland talked to Mama and explained everything to her. "Mrs. Harbinger, you must take the pills every day—without fail. Constance is in charge of your pills and will give them to you. If you take the pills, you'll feel better. Things will be easier for you. But, that will happen only if you take the pills. Do you understand?" he asked.

She nodded as she sat in the chair next to his desk, her fingers twisting in her lap. She looked so pathetic as she gazed up at him. In spite of all the times that she had hurt me physically and emotionally, my heart cried for the pain that she was experiencing at that moment.

That day, Mama began to take her medication. And, that very same day, her life began to turn around. The rages faded away, her temper was gone, and the tense look in her eyes, as well as the clenching of her jaw and the grinding of her teeth—they just disappeared. After a lifetime of horror and anguish, our lives began to change. Mama and Dad both seemed happier.

I was so pleased with Mama's progress. Our house was actually becoming a home—for the first time. Mama's attitude changed, her posture changed—even her voice changed. When I took Mama back to see Dr. Cortland, he was pleased with her progress.

"You just keep taking those pills, Mrs. Harbinger," he told her. "They're really helping you."

Each morning, I placed one of the pills in a small pink cup beside Mama's place at the table. Each morning, she took the pill after she'd finished her breakfast. I called them "magic pills" because of the difference that they'd made in my mother's life—and, therefore, in Dad's life and my life, too.

As the summer progressed, I was busier than usual—pulling weeds from the vegetable garden, and putting beans, beets, tomatoes, and apples into hot canning jars, which I carried down to the basement.

When Mama decided that she wanted the dining room painted,

we went together to pick out the color. It was actually fun to select just the right shade for the walls. Mama found a real bargain on material that would complement the new color. While I painted the walls, she made new drapes. Together, we'd created a whole new look in our dining room. We were so proud of our accomplishments. The best part of the whole experience, though, had been working with Mama. For the first time in my life, we'd been working as a team to turn a drab room into an attractive one.

Because I'd been so busy during those days, I'd often finished breakfast before Mama had. I'd hurried out to the garden—intent on tackling the persistent weeds before the heat of the day came pouring down on me.

A few weeks after we'd finished redecorating the dining room, Mama had the first tantrum that she'd had for a couple of months. She had been sitting on the back steps, husking corn from our garden. One moment, she'd been calmly stripping the ears of corn—and the next, she was hurling them out onto the lawn. The old, angry scowl was back on her face, her hands shook, and she was clenching and grinding her teeth.

I heard her almost snarl. I ran toward her—and then, I ran from her as she threw ears of corn at me. In a heartbeat, all the old terror that I'd known for a lifetime came crashing down upon me. What had gone wrong? Why had she begun to act that way? I tried again to approach her, but she screamed at me.

"Get away! Leave me alone!" she cried.

She stormed across the porch, went into the house, and slammed the screen door behind her. Inside, I could hear her throwing things. A dish smashed against a wall, and a heavy pot hit the floor. And, the screaming—that high-pitched yelling—it tore at my mind, causing my flesh to crawl.

I sat down on the porch step and cried. "Dear God," I prayed aloud. "Please, don't let me have to live through this again. Why is this happening again? I thought that the medicine was helping her. I give her the pills every day—why aren't they working?"

Hearing her raving inside the house terrified me. If the pills didn't control her, then what would? I was suddenly very afraid. Albert was no longer there to help me. And, something told me that Mama was even more of a danger to me at that moment than she'd ever been before. I knew in that moment that it was possible for her to hurt me very badly—or, even to kill me.

I wished that Dad were there to help me with Mama, but he'd left earlier to go to the next town for some supplies.

Moving like a blind person, I stumbled from the porch step and started down the driveway. I hurried across the road and went up on

Sadie Monroe's front porch. Before I could even knock on her door, it was opened and two hands had quickly pulled me inside.

I'd expected to see Sadie standing there—but, suddenly, I was staring into Gil's eyes. His was staring at me with such intensity. My heart was pounding so hard that I was sure he could hear it. I could tell that he knew just what was happening across the road. He'd heard my mother's screams again. He just reached out and pulled me close to him, and wrapped his strong arms around me.

In the shelter of his arms, I felt safe—distant from the woman who was yelling in the kitchen across the road. I started to cry then, and Gil comforted me.

"It's okay," he said soothingly. "I know—I heard her. I won't let her hurt you. I promised Albert that I would take care of you, and I will."

In that moment—and with those gently spoken words—I felt as though a change had begun to take place in my life. A part of me welcomed that change—but a part of me held back from it. There was still a part of me that wondered if the change would be a good thing—or would it bring even more heartache into my life.

I just stood there at Sadie Monroe's front door. I'd expected her to answer the door when I'd fled in terror from my parents' house across the road. Out there in the country, there were very few people to turn to for help. I knew that I was lucky that Sadie Monroe and her son, Gil, lived just across the road.

When Mama had suddenly gone in to one of her tantrums—after months of being free of them—I had been totally terrified. I'd thought that the pills that Dr. Cortland had prescribed for her had been helping to ease her rages, soothe her nerves, and calm her mind. She'd changed from the mother from hell into a caring woman who took pride in her house and her appearance—and, even in me.

But, that day, as she'd sat on the back porch husking corn, she'd begun hurling the ears of corn angrily out into the yard. She'd sat there, her shoulders rigid, her jaw tense, her teeth grinding. There had been a snarling sound coming from her throat. In a heartbeat, she'd gotten up and stomped into the kitchen. I'd heard her screaming, and then, I heard the sound of glass shattering as she'd thrown something across the kitchen. In an instant, she'd regressed back into the monster that terrified me.

I'd known a lifetime of abuse at my mother's hands. My, brother, Albert had been driven from our home because of her rages—the intense physical and verbal abuse. She'd ranted at him for anything that he did—or didn't, do. Nothing was ever good enough to suit her. We never knew what would set her off or make her come after us with that horrible, wooden spoon. She'd wrapped her fingers around its long handle and had swiped at Albert or me—and her aim had been deadly.

The last time, she'd smacked Albert with it as he'd run from the house and hidden in the upper part of the garage. I'd found him there later, and he'd been crying. He might have been eighteen and recently graduated from high school—but, at that moment, he'd looked like a defeated little boy. He'd vowed then that he would leave.

"I'm not staying here to be screamed at and pushed around," he'd told me vehemently. "I refused to be beaten one more time with that lousy, wooden spoon! I'm leaving! The first chance I get, I'm out of here!"

And, when the carnival had come to town, he'd left with them. He'd been gone for almost two years, and I'd never heard from him again. And, his silence had broken my heart. I still missed him so much.

Albert had been the only person that I'd had in the world. He and I had protected one other from Mama's rages as best we could. When we had been terrified by her, we'd raced around to the back of the garage and had climbed up into our secret hiding place. With our hearts pounding and tears in our eyes, we'd huddled together, trying to calm down after our mother's latest outburst. Then, after graduation from high school, Albert had just gone away. He couldn't stand it any longer—so he'd just left. And he'd left me all alone.

I'd remembered his last words to me—that if I was ever in trouble, I should know that I could trust Gil. He'd told me that I could depend upon Gil.

And, that was exactly what I had done. When the fury of my mother's rage had shattered my world once again, I'd turned and raced across the road onto Sadie Monroe's porch. I'd been surprised to have Gil open the front door—and, just as surprised at the way that he had pulled me into the house and then, into his arms. ***He held me for a moment longer and I could feel his heart pounding as we stood in a long embrace. I felt that our two hearts were beating as one.

Then, I stepped back, just outside the circle of his arms. I looked into his face and saw concern and compassion there. I wiped a shaking hand across my face. He reached up and brushed a tear from my cheek. Then, he led me into the kitchen where he motioned for me to sit down at the table. Next, he poured me a cup of coffee from a pot on his mother's stove.

"What happened?" he asked after he'd sat down across from me. "I thought that your mother was doing better. I haven't heard her yell and scream—or anything—for a long time now. Mom told me that Dr. Cortland had given your mother some pills to help her. I was so glad to see that they really were helping her."

18

I shook my head. "I don't know—I really don't understand what could have happened. I've been giving Mama the pills every morning without fail. And, they have been helping her—making her feel normal again, for the first time in years. But, suddenly, she's at it again—screaming."

Tears filled my eyes again. I didn't want to cry—not in front of Gil.

Gil reached across the table and placed his strong hands over mine. "Constance, this is all too much for you. You must be so afraid. Do you know what set your mother off this time? What made her start screaming?" he asked.

I shook my head. "Truthfully, I have no idea. She's been doing so well lately. The pills—they really do help her. I just don't—" My voice faltered.

"I wish Mom were here," Gil murmured. "She's better at these things than I am. But she went to a lecture with some friends. I have no idea when she'll be back."

I sat there, feeling so defeated and so frightened. When Gil moved his hands from mine, I wrapped my hands around the cup that he'd set in front of me. The warmth of the cup seemed to soothe me a little. I sipped at the drink, then set the cup back on the table.

"You can stay here as long as you need to," Gil told me.

"I can't do that," I protested. "I have to get back home—I have to see if Mama is okay. My father isn't home, so she's alone. Anything could happen to her." I stood up. "I'd better be leaving."

"I'm going with you," Gil insisted as he moved around to stand beside me "There's no way that I'm going to let you go back over to your house alone."

I could tell that he was determined—and I had to admit to myself that I felt a lot better about going back across the road with him beside me.

When we walked into our kitchen, I could see shattered pieces of glass on the floor. A jar of spaghetti sauce had been smashed, and there was blood red marinara sauce everywhere.

I didn't see Mama. "Where is she?" I wondered aloud.

"We'd better check on her," Gil told me as he followed me into the living room. We found Mama in there, lying on the couch.

When Gil walked up beside her, she didn't move. Cautiously, he bent over her, checking for a pulse. He stood up and turned to look at me.

"She's all right—just sleeping. I guess all that screaming exhausted her."

"What should I do?" I asked

"Put a blanket over her to keep her warm—and let her rest. She needs the rest."

I walked down the small hallway and into my parents' bedroom. I reached for an afghan that Mama always kept on the bottom of the bed. On the table by the bed, I saw a book, a pile of magazines, and a small cup. I wasn't sure what had made me glance at the cup, but when I did, I was stunned. The cup held a number of pills—the pills that Dr. Cortland had prescribed for my mother, to control her mood swings and tantrums.

Carrying the afghan into the living room, I draped it across her sleeping form. Just then, she looked so peaceful, so relaxed—nothing like the totally distraught woman who had been screaming and throwing things a little while earlier.

I motioned Gil to follow me as I led the way back into the kitchen. We sat down at the table and I showed him the cup with the pills inside.

"Those are her pills?" he questioned. "What are they doing in the cup?"

I went to the cupboard, reached up on the top shelf, and retrieved the pill bottle that I'd opened for her each morning. I counted the pills that were inside. The number was correct—it was exactly the right number.

Gil looked at me, his eyes telling me that he was stunned by what we had inadvertently discovered: Mama hadn't been taking her pills. She'd obviously waited until I'd left the kitchen and then, she'd put the pills into the cup in the bedroom.

"As long as she takes her medication she does very well," I told Gil. "Now, I understand why she lost it so badly today. The fact is, she has seemed a little distant for the past few days—rather withdrawn. But, I've been so busy that I haven't really paid that much attention to her. If I had, then maybe none of this would have happened. I didn't know that she'd stopped taking her medication."

After calling Dr. Cortland and telling him what had happened, I followed his advice and let her sleep. When she woke up, I promised him that I would give her one of her pills. From that point forward, I vowed that I would stand over her each morning and watch to see that she took her daily dosage.

Gil helped me clean up the mess in the kitchen. I thought that we'd never get the sauce cleaned up off the floor, but we did. By the time Mama woke up and Dad returned home, there was no sign of Mama's earlier outburst.

Gil stayed right there by my side that night. He sat both of my parents down and explained that what had happened had been caused my mother's refusal to take her medication. He was very gentle but firm with both of them when he told them that there was to be no repeat of what had happened that day. He informed them that he would be keeping an eye on things, and that he would know if Mama neglected to take her medication in the future.

# Chapter 7

Once Mama had begun taking her medication regularly, she became, once again, the pleasant woman that I'd come to know and enjoy. Nothing more was said about her efforts to go without her pills—but, in the back of my mind, I was haunted by the question: What if the nightmare happened again?

Gil started coming over frequently when he got off work at the factory. He'd stop by and help me in the garden. Or, he'd help my father with the many chores around the house. Eventually, he was spending more time at our place than he did at his own home. I enjoyed having him there, and he seemed to enjoy being with me. And, thankfully, he did lift a good deal of the work from my shoulders.

The more time that Gil and I spent together, the more special he became to me. Maybe we'd grown up together—and maybe I'd known him for a lifetime—but, suddenly, he was different. He had grown into fine man—a man who was gentle, caring, compassionate, and even funny. As we worked together in the garden, he'd tease me and make me laugh. He made my heart sing. He made me feel young—for the first time in my life.

Suddenly, each day centered on my waiting for Gil to finish his day at work so that he could come across the road to be with me. We took long rides in his old car. We stopped at a small diner close to town and had cups of too-hot cocoa and large pieces of the best apple pie in the world. Gil took me to movies and to the county fair. At the fair, he won a fuzzy stuffed puppy for me. And, he handed me a surprise package. When I opened it, I was shocked to see a beautiful ring with a sparkling diamond.

As we stood in the middle of the fair, Gil asked me to marry him. When I whispered that I would, he slipped the ring on my finger and pulled me into his arms. And, at that moment, my world was complete.

My parents thought that Gil was wonderful—they treated him like a son. In a way, I believed that they saw Gil as a replacement for Albert. When Gil asked me to marry him, my parents were delighted

We were married six months later at the little church in town that we'd both attended since childhood. It was just a small wedding— only my parents and Mrs. Monroe were there.

I'd wished desperately that Albert could have been there to share that special moment with me. We'd heard nothing from him since he'd left. I'd thought that I eventually would have gotten used to him being gone, but I hadn't. And, I had truly longed to have him with me when I'd married best friend.

But, even though he wasn't there, I knew in my heart that he would approve. I was positive that he would have thought that my becoming Mrs. Gil Monroe was the best thing that could have happened to me. And, I knew that I was truly blessed to have such a wonderful, caring man love me and want me to be his wife.

We'd discussed where we would live. We'd considered living with Gil's mother, or with my parents, and we'd talked about getting a place of our own. In the end, though, we decided to stay with my parents. Because of their various ailments, my parents had moved into an extra room on the first floor. Since there was a bathroom on both floors, they no longer had to use the steps to the second floor. The upper floor became our own space and gave us all the privacy that we needed.

The time that Gil and I spent alone was, indeed, special. We were so much in love, and he was always so gentle with me. He always put my needs and wants ahead of his own. And, that just made me love him even more—if that were possible.

And so, I was still living with my parents, but I had my own life apart from them—I was Gil's wife, and that took precedent over being my parents' daughter. But, I still did all I could to help them. I took care of the garden, and I worked very hard to keep the house neat and clean.

I had suggested to Gil that I get a job—at least, a part-time position to help with our finances. He'd insisted that I had more than enough to do because I not only took care of my parents' home, but I also spent time across the road with his mother. The more I got to know Sadie Monroe, the more I grew to love her. I could see why Gil had grown into the gentle, caring man that he was. It was because of the influence of the gentle, caring mother who had raised him.

Working at the factory, helping with his mother's property, and also working to maintain my parents' place, kept Gil very busy. He'd suggested to Dad that the old, wood-burning furnace be replaced, but Dad had refused.

"It's been there all these years, and it's still a good furnace. There's no need to replace something that still works," my father had told him.

So, the ugly old furnace had remained in the basement and I'd helped Gil make the trips into woods to haul loads of logs that we'd stack behind the garage. At times like those—when we were working together to pile up the logs, I missed my brother. Would I ever see Albert again?

Before I'd realized it, Gil and I had celebrated our first

anniversary. Our life wasn't perfect—living in someone else's house was not an ideal situation—but we were very happy together. I thanked the Lord every day for giving me such a wonderful husband.

I wasn't sure how long life would have gone on in the same sort of comfortable rut if Dad hadn't fallen and injured his leg. I couldn't understand what caused the fall until Dr. Cortland explained that Dad had suffered a small stroke. Consequently, he'd lost his balance and fallen.

He spent some of time in the hospital and, when he returned home, he was in a wheelchair. A few weeks later, Dad suffered another stroke. That one was severe and, when Dad left the hospital the next time, it was to be admitted into a nursing home, where he could receive the kind of care that his limitations required.

I feared that there might not be much time left for my father. I wanted my brother to have a chance to talk with Dad before it was too late. I understood that there was a great deal of hurt and pain left over from a childhood that had been too severe and often too harsh. But, I also knew that time had mellowed my parents, and that they were not the same abusive people that they'd once been. I wanted Albert to see them that way—to have a chance to see and talk with his father while he still could. And, I wanted Albert to see my mother—the woman that she'd become. She was very careful about taking her medication faithfully, and I marveled at the difference that it made in her. I wanted my brother to see Mama that way—so that, perhaps, it would erase some of my brother's scars.

Autumn turned to winter and, after all the howling wind and piles of snow, it was a welcome sight to see the first birds of springtime in our yard.

Dad was still in the nursing home—no better and no worse than the day when he'd first been admitted. I took Mama to see him a couple of times a week. The visits were short, because they tired both of my parents. Then, I would bring Mama back home and fix her a cup of tea while I began to do the laundry or prepare our dinner

One day seemed to drag into another. I tried to keep myself too tired and weary to think about all of our problems. Taking care of Mama's garden and taking care of Mama's house—plus, helping Sadie Monroe—was enough to keep me too exhausted to think. And, it kept me too tired to worry about my brother.

In spite of my taking care of two households and Gil's hectic schedule, we still managed to have a wonderful, fulfilling life of our own. When we were upstairs in our private world, as we had begun to consider it, we could push aside the concerns of Gil's mom's failing health, and the cares of dealing with my own parents, and just focus on one another.

Sometimes, I prepared special meals and brought them upstairs, where we shared them at a small table on which I'd spread a beautiful tablecloth. There, we enjoyed romantic candlelight dinners. Those were our most special times—we allowed nothing to intrude on the little world that we had created for ourselves.

# Chapter 8

Then, one day, Albert returned home. The day that he came back, everything changed—at least, for me.

I had been in the kitchen, setting the table for supper. Gil was over at his mother's, tending to some chore. Mama was in the living room, watching a television show. I moved automatically from the cupboard to the table and then to the stove, where I stirred the pot of stew that had been simmering all afternoon.

I was reaching into the refrigerator for lettuce to begin preparing the salad when I heard footsteps on the back porch. I knew that they weren't Gil's footsteps, but I knew that I'd heard them before—and, something about them made my heart start to pound.

I closed the refrigerator door quickly and turned around to see Albert standing at the back door. For a long moment, we stood there, just looking at each other. He was on one side of the screen door—I was on the other. After all that time, that screen door was all that separated me from my beloved brother.

"Can I come in?" he asked hesitantly.

"Yes! Get in here!" I hurried around the table and pulled the door open for him. Then we were in each other's arms. My brother was finally home! My heart was pounding and my mind was racing.

After a moment, I pulled back from him and stood looking at him. He had changed. His hair was uncombed. His face was dirty and streaks of sweat—and tears, I suspected—had made marks on his cheeks. He was wearing an old shirt but it was so filthy that I couldn't really tell what color it was. His jeans—well, I knew at a glance that they would be tossed into the trash. But, none of it mattered—to me, he looked wonderful.

Then, suddenly, Mama was coming into the kitchen. At the sight of her, Albert tensed and made a movement as though he intended to go back out the door. I stepped between him and the door. I knew that he was remembering Mama as she had once been—as the woman who had abused him, who had hit him so hard with that horrible wooden spoon. He had no idea of how she had changed. I wasn't going to let him out of the room until he'd had a chance to see that things were different there at home.

"It's okay, Albert," I whispered in his ear as he took a step backward. "Mama is fine now. It's okay."

His shoulders eased a little. I moved up beside him and put my arm through his. We stood together—brother and sister—facing our mother. One of us was afraid—the other knew that there was nothing to fear.

"Mama, look!" I cried happily. "Albert is home."

Mama could see that he was hesitant. She wisely did not move toward him. "Albert," she said with tears in her voice, "I'm so glad that you're here. I'm so glad that you're home." I knew that she wanted to grab him—just as I had done—and that she wanted to hold him close, but an instinct had told her to proceed slowly. So, she sat down on the nearest chair.

"Sit down, son," she said softly. "Constance, get him something to drink. There's fresh lemonade. Get him a glass of that."

I poured a tall glass of the lemonade and set it on the table. "Sit down, Albert," I invited as I pointed to the drink. He sat down opposite Mama. He took the glass and with trembling, dirt-encrusted hands, put it to his lips, and drank. He closed his eyes as he savored the cold lemonade.

We began to talk—Mama and Albert and me. We didn't push him. We didn't demand explanations about where he had gone or what he had done. None of that mattered. All that mattered was the fact that Albert was back with us.

# Chapter 9

Albert began talking, and it was as though he had so much to say—as though he'd been wanting to talk to someone for a long time. So, he sat and talked. He told how he'd gone with the carnival and traveled for some time with them. Then, he told us that he'd decided that he hadn't liked that way of life.

He also told us that in one of the small towns that he'd traveled to, he'd met a girl—Eileen. He'd fallen in love and had gotten married. Albert and Eileen had lived with her family, and Albert had worked for a construction company. They'd had a nice life, and they'd had a baby. Yes, he confided with a smile, he had a son—Tyler.

Then, he stopped talking. He just sat there. Mama and I waited for him to speak. We knew that we couldn't push him.

He sipped at his lemonade, then set the glass on the table and continued. He told us about the fire. It had been a cold, winter afternoon. He'd been at work, he explained. He'd promised Eileen that he'd be home on time—but he'd stopped at the convenience store for some milk and butter and some formula for little Tyler. That stop had taken longer than he'd planned. When he'd gotten home, it had been too late.

No one knew what had caused the fire. Eileen's parents had been visiting friends when the blaze had erupted. But, Eileen and Tyler had been trapped in the flames. They'd never had a chance of escaping.

"It was all my fault," Albert rasped, almost in a whisper.

"No, Albert," I said softly. "It wasn't your fault. We're so very sorry about Eileen and little Tyler—it's a terrible, horrible thing—a tragedy. But, it wasn't your fault."

"That's right, son," Mama assured him, in a gentle tone that I was sure he'd never heard from her before. "Albert, you couldn't help it that the fire started. It isn't your fault."

"Yes, it is!" he insisted. "If I hadn't stayed at the store so long, or, if I'd gotten home on time—then it wouldn't have happened."

"You couldn't have known that there would be a fire," I pointed out. "You didn't start it—and, you couldn't have prevented it. It isn't your fault. You weren't even there."

"That's exactly right," he agreed sharply. "I wasn't there! If I had been there, I could have at least gotten Eileen and Tyler out of that house. It's my fault!"

As he concluded his story, Albert began to sob. Tears streaked down his dirt-encrusted face. There was no sound—just the tears.

Again, I heard footsteps on the back porch. Then, suddenly, Gil was in the room. He was startled to see Albert sitting at the table— but a glance at Mama and me warned him to proceed cautiously. He walked over and patted my brother on the back.

"Hey, Albert, I'm glad that you're back with us. You got here just in time to have some of Constance's famous stew."

Albert looked up and, in an instant, he'd gotten to his feet and wrapped his arms around his old friend. Gil stood there holding onto my brother, welcoming him back home.

# Chapter 10

The rest of that day was a blur of action and emotion. Albert began to relax when he realized how overjoyed we were to have him back with us. He was surprised at the gentle demeanor of our mother—she was nothing like the woman that he'd run away from. He was also surprised to learn that Dad was living at a nursing home. Albert was thrilled that Gil and I had gotten married and were living there with Mama.

Mama told him that he could have his old room back and, in a motherly manner, she told him to go take a shower and get cleaned up. She reminded him that there were still some of his clothes in his closet and in his chest of drawers.

"Hurry up!" Gil ordered good-naturedly. "We're going to be eating soon and if you aren't down here, you might not get any of this stew!"

While Albert was getting cleaned up, Mama and I told Gil about all that we'd just learned. I saw tears in my husband's eyes when he heard about the loss of Albert's wife and child.

He shook his head in disbelief. "That's horrible—just horrible."

It took several days for Albert to begin to relax and to feel that he was back home—in a home that was finally safe from terror. He still saw that house as the place where he'd known such fear and anguish, back when Mama had mistreated him. But, with each passing day, he saw more evidence of the change in our mother. I saw that he was beginning to trust her. For the first time, he didn't recoil in horror when she was around him.

After Albert had been back home for a few weeks, Gil asked him if he was planning to get a job.

"I know that there are several openings at the factory right now," Gil told my brother. "I'm sure that you'd have no trouble getting work there."

"No way!" Albert snapped. "I vowed years ago that I'd never work at the factory. I meant what I said."

His blunt attitude had obviously shocked Gil, but my husband didn't say anything. "That's okay," Gil soothed. "No problem. You don't have to work at the factory if you don't want to. There should be other work available around here."

Albert didn't even respond to that—he just got up and walked out of the house. A few minutes later, I saw him walking along the road—moving with quick, jerking steps. There was something very wrong with the way that he moved and with his posture. Seeing him that way sent a twinge of fear down my spine.

The outburst from Albert hadn't really surprised me. I'd noticed the same reaction from him a number of times over the past few days. He seemed so tense all the time—he couldn't sit and watch television for more than a few moments. He would be up out of his chair—going to the kitchen for a glass of water or can of soda—or, for nothing. Then, he'd return to the living room, drop deliberately into his chair, give a deep sigh, and sit facing the television screen—but not seeing it. He held the newspaper in his hands but never turned the pages. He just sat there, holding the newspaper—sometimes it was a week-old edition. But, it didn't matter what issue it was, because he never even looked at it.

Albert would get up from the couch or the kitchen table, hurry from the room, move quickly out the back door, and head down the driveway. Then, he'd walk up and down the road, taking odd, scuffling steps. His shoulders would be hunched, and his hands would be stuffed down into his pockets. He looked as though he were lost— totally lost.

When Mama or Gil were around, Albert put on a good front. It almost seemed as though he were doing very well. He sat out on the back porch with Gil in the evenings and they chatted, sharing casual, comfortable conversation. And, eventually, Albert sat in the living room and talked with Mama as she mended clothing or watched television. When they were around, he had one demeanor—one manner. But, when they weren't around, he was a totally different person. When it was just the two of us, he would snarl and snap order at me.

"Get me more coffee, Constance! Can't you see that my cup is almost empty?" he'd snarl. "And, next time, don't make the coffee so strong. I could take the paint off the garage door with this stuff!"

# Chapter 11

Every day, Gil ate breakfast early and headed off to work. Mama ate next—just some cereal and toast. Then, she left the kitchen to go watch television or to work on her mending or to read. When Albert came into the kitchen, I could feel the muscles in the back of my shoulders start to tighten. What would I do wrong that time?

It didn't take me long to find out. Albert would drop onto the nearest chair, prop his elbows on the table, and start barking at me.

"Constance, where's my breakfast! What does a guy have to do to get some decent food around here!" he'd snap.

I hurried to fix him pancakes or sausage or eggs—whatever he asked. But, no matter what I did, it was always wrong. The eggs were not cooked properly or the pancakes were burned. Or, he'd complain that the bacon wasn't crisp enough—it was always something.

He started following me around the house—just trailing along behind me, watching everything that I did, and every move that I made. He'd mutter things under his breath.

"She doesn't even know how to run the vacuum or dust. She takes so long to wash a few dishes. She doesn't know how to sweep the kitchen floor."

Sometimes, he stood in the doorway of whatever room I was working in. He'd just stand there, arms outstretched. If I wanted to get past him, he wouldn't let me through. He was deliberately blocking the doorway.

Then, suddenly, he became more aggressive. If I tried to go through a doorway, he would shove me. He pushed me into the kitchen table, and into the sharp corner of the table in the dining room.

After I'd straightened up the clutter that he always left in the living room—newspapers and magazines all left in total disarray by him—he'd grab the neat pile of magazines on the coffee table and "accidentally" send them crashing to the floor. Then, he'd stand there looking at me—defying me, daring me to complain. I said nothing. I just reached down, picked up the magazines, and set them slowly back onto the coffee table.

I'd mentioned some of this behavior to Gil, but he just brushed it aside.

"Constance, you have to be patient with Albert. He's been through so much—the loss of his wife and baby. It's been so hard for him. It took a lot of courage for him even to come back home. I never thought that we'd see him again. But he's here, and that's a good sign.

You have to be patient with him—give him time," he told me gently.

"But, Gil, I'm really concerned," I insisted. "I'm worried about Albert. Something is seriously wrong with him. I'm afraid—" I broke off, my voice trembling.

Gil pulled me close into he circle of his arms. "Constance, honey, be patient. Albert will be just fine. Give him time to adjust. Just be grateful that your brother has come home. Everything will be all right—in time."

But, I knew things that neither Mama nor Gil knew. I knew that Albert was prone to rages and mood swings. I knew that he could be violent. I'd seen him a few days earlier when he'd been walking jerkily along the road. Just seeing him moving like that had sent chills down my spine. But, when I saw what he did to old Mr. Potter's dog—well, that really frightened me.

Mr. Potter lived down the road. He was elderly and alone, except for a weary old dog named Ivan. Ivan sometimes wandered down the road and strolled into our yard. I gave him a few scraps of meat or some day-old bread. He ate whatever I offered him, wagged his tail, meandered down the driveway, and headed back home. He'd been doing that since before Albert had left.

But, one morning, I glanced out the window and saw Albert scuffling along the road. He was going nowhere—just walking. Then, as I saw Ivan come strolling down the road, I smiled. I knew that it would be the first time that Albert would have seen Ivan since he'd left with the carnival. I was sure that he'd be glad to see his old friend. I recalled the way that Ivan had followed Gil and Albert whenever they'd gone fishing. I was pleased that Ivan had come along, thinking that maybe it would help Albert to see the dog that he'd loved so much. As Ivan approached Albert on his old-dog legs, he was wagging his scruffy tail. I could tell he was glad to see Albert.

The next instant, my heart stopped! From the window, I saw Albert lift his foot and kick Ivan. A harsh, deliberate movement caught the aged, friendly dog right behind the ribs. The impact of the kick was so strong that Ivan was hurled through the air and landed in the roadside ditch. I could hear his frantic yelps.

I ran as fast as I could. I ran out the door and down the driveway. I found Ivan lying on his side—blood beginning to seep from his open mouth. His beautiful eyes looked up at me through a cloud of pain and disbelief. His body was broken, but worse than that, I knew that his heart was broken—to think that someone he'd considered his friend had done such a thing to him.

I looked in the direction that Albert had headed. He was gone. I realized that he must have gone off the road and into the woods. I screamed his name, but there was no response.

I turned my attention to Ivan. In that instant, I knew that there was nothing I could do for him. I sat down right in the ditch with him, held his head on my lap, and stroked him as he breathed his last. I cried so hard over the loss of my faithful, four-legged neighbor.

I left Ivan there—out of the way of what little traffic we did have on that deserted back road. I had to go to the house to call Mr. Potter and tell him about Ivan.

When I got to my kitchen, my heart heavy with grief, Albert was sitting there. The look on his face terrified me. He looked so calm, so composed—and yet, he looked totally lethal.

"Why did you do that?" I demanded as I wiped at my tears. "Why did you kick Ivan? You knew how much Ivan loved you!"

"Me? Kick Ivan?" He laughed—a sort of odd-sounding, odd-pitched laugh. "I never kicked anyone. Ivan was hit by a car. Too bad." He shrugged.

"But, Albert, I saw you kick Ivan—right over into the ditch. He's dead, Albert—and you did it!"

"Constance, I did nothing of the sort. There is nothing to tell—nothing. Do you understand me?" Albert spoke very slowly, very softly—very deliberately.

In an instant, Albert was up out of his seat, standing right in front of me. The glare on his face, his heavy breathing, and his fists clenched rigidly at his sides—he terrified me! If he could kick an innocent helpless dog, a dog that he'd once loved, what else was he capable of doing?

What would Albert do to me? At that moment, I knew the brother that I loved was capable of harming me—and, possibly, killing me. But, I also knew that neither Mama nor Gil would believe me. They only saw the good side of him. I, alone, had seen the evil side of my brother. And, what I had seen had caused my blood to run cold. After seeing what he had done to Ivan, I wondered if I would be his next victim.

I was still amazed at the two sides to my brother. When he was around Mama or Gil, he was quiet and cordial. In fact, he seemed like the Albert that we'd all known before he'd left home several years earlier.

There was a tension in the house, an ever-present feeling of wondering what Albert would say or do next. I tried to be patient with him, tried to give him time and space to deal with his problems. Gil didn't have to witness much of what I saw during the day because in the evening, Albert seemed to be on his best behavior—and I knew that it was because Gil was home from work.

I was concerned about my brother's well-being. He spent too

much time sitting and brooding, saying nothing—just staring off into space. I felt he needed to have something to keep him busy—help fill his time. When I repeated Gil's previous suggestion that Albert see about getting work at factory, he went wild with rage.

"Can't you people hear? I told you that I will not work there! No way! And that's the end of the subject!" he exclaimed.

"Did you know they're building a new housing development out near the highway?" I informed him. "I'll bet that you could get on one of those work crews. You are really good with that kind of work. Maybe you—"

"Shut up!" He spun around and glared at me. "Just close that big mouth of yours! I am not going to work on some dumb crew that is building some dumb housing development out by the dumb highway!"

Then, he hurried out the back door and stormed across the back porch. Through the kitchen window, I could see him moving rapidly toward the woods. I knew that he would walk among the trees for an hour or so. When he returned, I knew that he might be calmed down— maybe. At least, I hoped that he would be.

Again, when Gil got home from work, Albert was cordial. He sat on the back porch and had easy conversation with Gil while I put the finishing touches on dinner. The meal went well. Mama enjoyed the ham that I'd prepared, and Gil had second helpings of scalloped potatoes. Even Albert asked for another piece of the cherry pie that I'd baked that afternoon.

We all sat in the living room that evening, watching a movie on television. When the program had ended, Mama went to bed and Albert went upstairs to his room. That left Gil and me, alone in the living room. I realized that we hadn't had many times alone during the past days and weeks. It was so nice to just sit there quietly at the end of a busy day and relax together.

I mentioned to Gil that Albert still didn't want to get a job. "When I suggested it to Albert today, he got really angry with me," I informed my husband. "He yelled and stormed out of the house. I'm concerned about him."

"Give him time, Constance. Don't push him. Losing his wife and baby has been rough on him. He'll be okay in time."

"But he seems so hostile at times," I said hesitantly. "Sometimes, he—"

"I think that you're pushing him too hard. You need to back off," Gil interrupted. "Let him come to terms with things at his own pace." He gently rubbed his hand up and down my arm and then pulled me closer to him. "Let's forget about Albert for now. It seems that he's all you talk about these days. How about talking about us—just you and

35

me? That is my favorite subject, you know."

I said nothing more about my brother as I melted into the tender embrace of my wonderful husband

# Chapter 12

The next morning, just after Gil had left for work, Albert came into the kitchen.

"Are you going to fix me some breakfast?" he asked sharply.

His tone had startled me. I glanced up from the table where I had been sitting and having a second cup of coffee. Something about Albert didn't look right. He hadn't combed his hair, and he was wearing the same shirt he'd worn for the past three days. And, he'd sort of swaggered into the room.

A warning bell went off in my mind. Something wasn't right there. But, still, I smiled at him, set down my cup, and went over to the stove.

"I'll be glad to fix your breakfast for you," I told him as I placed the skillet on the stove. "How many eggs do you want? And how do you want them? Fried? Scrambled?"

"You and your stupid questions! Fix them the way I want them!" he demanded.

Not really knowing how he wanted them prepared, and knowing that if I didn't do it right I would face his anger, I set about fixing him scrambled eggs—making them just the way that Mama had prepared them for him when he was a kid. Then, I made some toast, poured him a cup of hot coffee, and set a glass of juice in front of him.

"You call these scrambled eggs?" he scoffed as he tackled the food on his plate. "And this toast—how can you burn toast like this?" he asked as he held up a perfectly golden slice of toast.

"I'm sorry if I prepared the food incorrectly, Albert," I told him as I stood at the sink washing out the skillet. "Would you like for me to fix you something else?"

"Forget it! If you can't get this food right, what makes you think that you can get anything else right?" He threw a slice of toast onto the floor and shoved his chair back so hard that he shook the table, causing coffee to spill out of his cup. Seeing the coffee spilled on the table, he headed toward me. "See what you made me do, Constance?" he growled. "You made me spill my coffee!"

I turned from the sink in time to see him moving toward me. The look in his eyes frightened me. Who was that man? He certainly was not my dear brother. The man in front of me was a stranger, and I was afraid of him. Instinctively, I held the skillet in front of me—not as a threat to him, but as protection for myself.

The next instant, Albert turned and hurried out the back door. I saw him heading down the driveway toward the road. I knew that he would pace up and down the dusty, rutted road for a few hours. Well, I figured that at least he would be out of the house for a while. He wouldn't be a threat to me.

That evening, Gil and I walked out to the garden so that I could show him how well the plants were progressing. After admiring my abilities as a gardener, Gil turned to me.

"You work too hard around here, honey. You do all the housework and you go across the road and help Mom, too. Plus, you take such wonderful care of this garden. It's a lot of work—I know that. Maybe you can get Albert to help with the garden. At least, that would take some of the burden off of you."

"I don't think that Albert would help me," I said hesitantly.

"Why not?" Gil asked. "He has nothing else to do. He has no job to go to. He could help with tending the garden."

"Albert hates gardening," I reminded Gil. "You know that as little kids you and he used to do everything you could to get out of helping with the garden." I started to laugh. "I remember one time, when Dad asked Albert to pull the weeds, you and he took off into the woods and hid up in a tree to get out of doing it. Guess who had to yank out those weeds?" I grinned. "Me—as always."

Gil chuckled. "Yes, I remember that time. We actually sat up in a tree on the edge of the woods and watched you pulling those weeds."

"You guys!" I laughed as I swatted playfully at his arm.

"But, seriously," Gil said as his mood changed, "I don't see why Albert can't help you in some way. It would give him something to do."

"Gil, you don't really know Albert," I insisted as I turned to look at the road where my brother was once again walking slowly along, his shoes scuffling the dust as he took each step. "Albert has become so moody. He gets angry, he's belligerent, and he's—"

"Constance," Gil interrupted. "I think that you're exaggerating the situation. I've known Albert all my life. He's none of those things. I think that you're seeing problems that don't exist. Albert is a nice guy. He's had some bad luck, and he needs time to get over it."

"I'm with Albert all day," I reminded Gil. "I see things that you don't see."

"Well, I'm with Albert in the evenings," my husband countered, "and I see none of the things that you are accusing him of. He seems kind of quiet, but that's understandable. He'll be fine—in time." Then, he gave me a stern look. "Especially if you leave him alone and give him some space."

Gil stood there staring at me for a moment and I could see that he was thinking—considering something. After hesitating for a moment, he began to speak again.

"You know, I think that I'm beginning to see a pattern here," he said quietly.

"A pattern?" I asked, bewildered.

"Yes. I don't mean to upset you, but I can see some of your mother's old ways in you. She always used to find fault with Albert. No matter what he did, it was wrong. He used to tell me all about it when we were kids. And now, I think that I'm seeing that same trait starting to emerge in your attitude toward him," he told me.

I just stood there, absolutely stunned. I couldn't believe what my husband had just said to me. He thought that I was turning into the woman my mother had once been, when Albert and I were kids. Gil truly thought that everything was my fault, and that all of the problems had been caused by my negative attitude toward my brother.

I wanted to defend myself. I wanted to tell Gil that he had everything all wrong. But, I could tell from the look on his face that he really believed what he had just said to me. He thought I was becoming a nagging person—a person who constantly picked at Albert.

I turned and walked away from the garden, moving slowly toward the house. I didn't wait to see if Gil followed me. Actually, I didn't want to see or talk to him just then. My heart was still pounding from the shock of the startling statement that I'd just heard from my husband. As I went up onto the back porch, I glanced toward the road. Gil and Albert were standing there talking and laughing—just like best friends.

# Chapter 13

Because of the tension that I dealt with all day, by the time Gil and I went to bed at night, I often was exhausted and still tied in knots. I couldn't relax and I had trouble sleeping. I didn't want to keep Gil awake with my tossing and turning. I knew that he had to have his rest because he had to go to work the next day. I started going down to the living room, where I'd sit in the recliner. Sometimes, I dozed off down there. It wasn't the most comfortable way to sleep, but it assured me that my husband was getting the proper rest.

I missed being beside him during the night. I missed having him reach out to me at the start of a new day. Still, I felt it was best for Gil to get a good night's uninterrupted sleep—so I spent more and more nights down in the living room—alone.

Our lives might very well have continued in the same pattern for months had it not been for the thunderstorm. I'd always liked thunderstorms, but even as a child, Albert had been afraid of them. That storm was really a dramatic one—lots of thunder and lightening, with torrents of rain hurling down from the sky. Albert paced the living room like a caged animal as the storm raged outside.

Suddenly, a bright bolt of lightening lit up the sky and in an instant, the lights in our house went dead. A power line somewhere nearby must have been hit. Since it was Saturday, Gil was home from work. He routinely went through the house, checking to make sure that everything was secure. I got emergency candles from the cupboard and put a flashlight in my pocket—just in case. They were just routine actions—nothing unusual. After making sure things that were all right at our house, Gil headed across the road to check on his mother.

As soon as Gil left the house, Albert came into the kitchen where I stood, washing some dishes.

"See what you did?" he yelled.

"What?" I turned from the sink to see him standing in the doorway, his hair disheveled, his shirt pulled out of the waistband of his jeans. The look in his eyes sent a chill down my spine. I didn't know the person who was standing before me—he was not my brother.

"See what you did!" he yelled again.

"What I did?" I asked. "What are you talking about? I didn't do anything."

"You made the lights go out! That's what you did!"

"Albert, the storm downed a power line. The lights will be on soon. I—"

Before I could say anything more, he lunged toward me. "I want light! And I want it now!" he screamed.

Things began to move in slow motion then. I heard myself talking softly to him as I inched my way from the sink to the table. He followed me. I managed to keep the table between us. My heart was pounding, and my throat felt dry. Who was that crazed man before me? What was wrong with him? I was terrified. I wished that Gil were there, but I knew he would be at his mother's house for some time. I was alone in that horrifying nightmare.

A part of my mind seemed to go numb, but I did manage to consider my mother's safety. I knew that she was in her bedroom, taking a nap. With her door closed, she might not even have heard Albert raving at me. As long as she was in there, I was sure that she would be safe. Also, I did not think my brother would risk harming her—he was still somewhat afraid of her. But, I was sure that he could harm me—if he got the chance. I wasn't dealing with a rational person. I was dealing with my own brother—who had become a total stranger to me.

Lord, please help me, I prayed silently. Tell me what to do.

Suddenly, I knew what to do to defend myself. I stepped over to the cupboard, opened a drawer, and grabbed at the old wooden spoon that Mama had used so often, years before. The handle was worn smooth by having been held so often as she'd threatened us when we were kids. Her accuracy when she'd smacked at us with that spoon had been deadly. It was a small object but it had caused both of us such enormous pain.

Years later, I held that wretched spoon and, somehow, just the feel of it gave me the courage to make my next move. I spun around, held up the wooden spoon, and waved it at my brother.

"Albert, you stop right there!" I ordered. "Just stop!"

To my amazement, he stopped instantly. He stood there, looking at that spoon. Then, he put one hand on his arm and rubbed. It was as though he were remembering when that spoon had landed with striking blows on his arms and shoulders.

"Go sit down, Albert!" I snapped. I'd had no idea if he would do as I'd said, but he'd pulled out a kitchen chair and sat down obediently. "Now, stay there!" I told him coldly.

I walked past him, still holding up the wooden spoon. I got a good look at his eyes and what I saw there was a horrible dullness— an anguish. It broke my heart to see that look in my brother's eyes. I knew that the terrible loss of his wife and his baby had pushed him too far—and it was the loss that was causing him to behave in such a terrible way. The Albert that I had grown up with would never have screamed at me—would never have yelled at me. Knowing how deep and profound his heartbreak was made my heart ache for him. But, I had to push aside those feelings and concentrate on the moment. I had to protect myself, and I had to protect my mother. Oh, how I wished that Gil was there!

With one glance at Albert's face and eyes, I knew that he was dangerous. What should I do? I slowly backed out of the kitchen. Moving into the living room, I grabbed at a sheet of paper on the coffee table. Using the pen that Mama used to write her grocery lists, I scribbled a note.

Mama—Albert is dangerous! I wrote. Lock your door and stay in your room.

Then, I signed my name, went to Mama's door, and slid the note under the door—hoping that when she woke up, she would find it before she opened her door and stepped out of her room.

I heard Albert moving around in the kitchen. I wasn't sure if I should go back in there and see how he was. I already knew the answer to that, though. My brother was definitely not all right. I also knew that my very life was in danger if I stayed there one moment longer. Pulling my jacket from the closet, I threw it over my shoulders and headed out the front door.

The rain had stopped and the early evening had a fresh, clean feel to it. My heart, however, had a soiled, corroded feeling to it. I trodded through the wet grass and headed around the side of the house toward the garage. I knew that I could hide in there for a little while.

Standing just inside the wide door, I kept looking at the house. There was still enough daylight so that I could see through the kitchen window. I could see Albert pacing back and forth near the sink.

Please, Lord, I prayed. Please, let Gil come home. I am so afraid of Albert.

My heart began to pound when I saw Albert open the back door and step out onto the porch. Did he know where I was? Was he coming to get me? What should I do?

Dear Lord, I prayed silently. Tell me what to do.

I huddled in the shadows of the garage and watched as Albert started off the porch. Then, I saw him tramp through the mud toward the garage. I watched as he turned suddenly, walked back up onto the porch, and went into the house.

The moment he was out of sight, I ran from my hiding place, raced around to the back of the garage, and scrambled up the stack of wood. I wondered if the window would still open. I was afraid that time and humidity might have sealed the window. But, when I gave a hard shove, it opened. I climbed in, dropped onto the floor, and stood there, trying to catch my breath from the effort of climbing up the pile of wood and forcing the window open.

Cautiously, I moved across the rough floorboards of the storage room above the garage. I had to step carefully by some of the lumber and tools that Dad had stored there so long ago.

A second window opposite the one that I'd just climbed through gave me a view of the back of the house, into the kitchen window. I could see Albert moving about in the kitchen. I wasn't sure how long I stood there. My legs were shaking and my heart was pounding. But, gradually, I began to calm down a little. I knew that I had to focus. While there was still some daylight, I had to assess my situation.

No one knew where I was. There was an advantage to that—it meant that Albert didn't know where to find me. But, it also meant that Gil didn't know where to find me, either.

Standing alone in the dusty room, I glanced around, trying to determine what to do. I spied the old crate that had been pushed up against the wall. It had once held Albert's supplies—his provisions for the day when he would leave home. The night before he'd left home, we had sat together on that crate. It was where he'd told me of his plans to leave the next day with a traveling carnival. I'd hoped that he wouldn't really go—but when I'd woken up the next morning, he'd been gone.

I pulled the crate closer to the window, used a tissue from my pocket to swipe at the layers of dirt, and sat down. From there, I could see the kitchen quite well.

Suddenly, I saw Albert walking out of the house again. He was heading right for the garage. Would he come into the garage? Did he somehow know that I was there? Did he remember that it had once been our refuge? Would he climb up and try to find me? And, if he did, what would he do to me? I had loved my brother so much when we were children—but, suddenly, I feared him so much. I couldn't even pray for help because my mind was too terrorized to form a prayer.

"Constance! Constance! Where are you!" Albert screamed—and his tone warned me that if he did find me, he would, indeed, harm me. I didn't answer him, but I was certain that the pounding of my heart was loud enough for him to hear as he moved through the door.

"You are going to be sorry!" Albert bellowed as he moved about, just below the floor where I was trying to be silent—and totally invisible. "You know how much I hate storms! I hate it when the lights go out! Why did you do that to me, Constance?" He lowered his voice menacingly. "You are going to be sorry that you did that to me." The softer tone was even more threatening than his screeching had been.

I could hear him throwing things—tools that Gil kept neatly on the garage wall were being tossed about. Several of them hit Gil's car with the crashing sound of metal striking metal.

Then, the noise stopped. Suddenly, it was too quiet. What was Albert doing? Maybe he'd left the garage. I hoped and prayed that he had. Maybe he had headed back toward the house—but, in order for me to see if he had, I knew that I would have to move closer to the window. If I did that, Albert might hear my footsteps on the floor above his head, and then, he would know where I was. I sat perfectly still, afraid to move from the box. Any movement might cause the box to make a scraping sound on the floor and that would reveal my hiding place.

All the time in the universe hung suspended by a very weak thread. I had never been so afraid in my life.

Then I heard the very sound I had feared most: Albert was trying to climb the ladder that hung suspended from the hole in the garage ceiling. How many times had my brother and I descended down that old ladder after we'd been hiding up there? Of course, Albert knew where I was! He'd known that the one place I would run for refuge was that disgusting, dark room. And, now he was starting to climb the ladder to get to me.

"I'm going to get you, Constance!" he yelled. "All those years when Mama hit me and screamed at me—it was all your fault! And, now it's your fault, too. You are going to be so sorry." The ladder groaned under my brother's weight.

Just when I felt certain that I would faint from terror, I heard a shout. Through the rain-smeared window, I saw Gil coming out onto the back porch. He was calling to Albert, trying to coax him back inside. I could tell by his tone that he knew what was happening. He'd obviously returned from his mother's house, had sized up the situation, and was trying to deal with it. Finally, he'd realized the truth and was trying to protect Mama and me from Albert, who was totally out of control.

Gil moved toward the garage. I could hear the two men in the garage right underneath me. Gil was talking softly to Albert—trying to get him to go into the house. But, Albert did not intend to do that. I heard a scuffle and the sound of men grunting and moaning as they landed blows on one another. I knew that Gil was strong from hard, physical work—but I also knew that anyone in a rage could have superhuman strength. It was possible that Albert could kill my husband!

The struggle seemed to go on for an eternity. Then, suddenly, Gil was running toward the house. I saw him go into the house, and then, I saw him standing in the kitchen, using his cell phone. I knew that he was calling for help.

I could hear Albert in the room beneath me. He was moaning and muttering inaudible words. Then, an ambulance arrived, and men in hospital garb were running to the garage. Right under my feet, I heard them talking to Albert, reassuring him that everything would be okay. Suddenly, he was gone—taken out to the ambulance and driven away just as a new rainstorm began.

At last, I knew that it was safe for me to leave my hiding place. I moved toward the ladder, put my foot on the top rung, and almost fell to the garage floor as the worn ladder broke loose and crashed in splinters, right where Albert and Gil had stood, arguing, just a short while before.

How was I going to get out of there? There was no way that I could climb back out the rear window and down the pile of wood. The rain had made it entirely too slippery. I sat on the box and started to cry. I felt so defeated—so alone. That room had to be the most horrible place in the world, and I hated being there.

How long had I been up there? Taking the flashlight from my pocket, I turned it on and glanced at my watch. I'd been up there almost an hour. I had to get out of there before I lost my mind. I knew that I could use the flashlight, since Albert was no longer a threat. I looked about, trying to determine how to climb out of the room safely. But, no matter how hard I concentrated, I couldn't think of a solution. Again, I sat down on the box and cried.

Gil didn't know that I was up there. Mama didn't know I was there. Only Albert knew—and he was gone. At least, he was no longer a threat to me, I realized as I huddled on the box. I felt chills go through my body. The rain had started again and a damp wind blew in through the open garage door and drifted up to wrap like a shroud around me. I closed my eyes, wrapped my arms around myself, and sobbed.

"Hey! What are you doing up there?" Gil's voice caused me to jerk around and glance down through the hole in the floor. There he stood, holding a large flashlight. He was looking up at me and grinning, but there were tears streaming down his face.

He quickly moved an extension ladder close to the edge of the hole in the floor. "Think you can climb down now?" he asked.

In an instant, I was down—out of the terror of that storage room. I was locked in his arms and I cried—tears of relief that I was finally safe.

"How's Mama?" I asked.

"She's fine," Gil assured me. "And Albert is going to be fine—in time. He's been taken to the hospital for observation."

My protective husband kept his arm around me as we scurried across the yard through the rain. Soon, I was seated at the kitchen table with a cup of hot tea that Mama had given me. She seemed fine—a little shaken by all that had happened, but basically fine. She'd seen the note that I'd slipped under her door and had stayed locked in her bedroom until Gil had come home. She had been able to tell him about Albert so that my husband had been alerted to the danger waiting in the kitchen. Gil had told Mama to go back into her room and lock the door again, which she'd done until the danger had been over.

"How did you know that I was in the upper storage room in the garage?" I asked Gil as I took a sip of the hot tea.

"At first, I didn't know where you were. I was scared to death that Albert had hurt you in some way. I searched the house but there was no sign of you. I was in the kitchen, ready to call the police, when I saw your flashlight through the upstairs garage window," he told me with a smile. "I remembered that you and Albert used to hide up there years ago. I also knew about the ladder because Albert and I had used it to get down out of that room when we were kids. But, when I got to the garage to get you, the ladder was broken."

"Well, you rescued me," I told him gratefully. "If it hadn't been for you, I might still be up there."

"Well, you're safe now—and that's all that matters," Gil said tenderly

# Chapter 14

That rainy night was a turning point for all of us. The doctors told us that Albert was suffering from the shock of losing his wife and baby. He remained hospitalized for a couple of months.

When he was discharged and allowed to return home, Dr. Cortland set up a counseling schedule for Albert. My brother willingly attended the sessions and, with the help of a compassionate therapist, he began to come to terms with his loss. He gradually accepted the fact that nothing would ever bring Eileen and little Tyler back to him—but he also realized that their deaths were not his fault. He finally began to find closure about that.

Dr. Cortland also told us that Albert suffered from the same chemical imbalance that Mama had experienced for so many years. The trauma of losing Eileen and little Tyler had triggered the malady that had lain dormant within Albert for so long. Now, with the help of proper medication and the love of his family, my brother is making progress toward becoming the special young man that I remember.

I want my brother to be as happy as I am with my wonderful, adoring husband. Last year, Gil and I became proud parents of a beautiful little girl who we named Sadie, after her grandmother. Dad passed away a few months after Albert's return home from the hospital. I was pleased that he and Albert had a chance to get to know one another again.

There have been some changes at my mother's house—the old garage has been torn down and replaced with a newer structure. And, the old wood-burning furnace has been replaced with an efficient gas furnace. There is no more need for a woodpile.

Today, I thank the Lord for the two special men in my life—my gentle brother and my adoring husband.

THE END